Abando

"Well, I think we can safely say that Mr Harding's not going to come for Jessie tonight," Bob Parker announced late that evening. "I've just tried the phone number he gave us. I got the 'number unobtainable' sound, so I checked with the operator. It's 'out of order', according to her."

Neil bit his lip. Should he tell his dad what he and Kate had found out about Harding's address?

For the moment he decided to keep quiet. He wanted to work it out himself, and with everything else that had happened, the matter of 149 Dale End Road had slipped his mind. Anyway, they had all felt so positive that Harding *would* be back to pick up Jessie.

"What do we do now, then?" Neil enquired.

"Wait to see if he turns up tomorrow. His flight's probably been delayed."

Neil hoped his father was right – that it wasn't anything more serious than that . . .

Titles in the Puppy Patrol *series*

More Puppy Patrol stories follow soon

Puppy Patrol
Abandoned!

Jenny Dale

Illustrated by
Mick Reid

A Working Partners Book
MACMILLAN CHILDREN'S BOOKS

Special thanks to Linda Kempton

First published 1997 by Macmillan Children's Books
a division of Macmillan Publishers Limited
25 Eccleston Place, London SW1W 9NF
and Basingstoke

Associated companies throughout the world

Created by Working Partners Limited
London W6 0HE

ISBN 0 330 34907 4

11 13 15 17 16 14 12

A CIP catalogue record for this book is available from
the British Library.

Typeset in Bookman Old Style
Printed and bound in Great Britain by Mackays of Chatham plc, Kent

Chapter One

It was half past eight in the evening when a loud knock on the Parkers' front door startled everyone.

Sam barked noisily and ran into the hallway. Five-year-old Sarah stamped after him, giggling excitedly.

"I'll get it!" laughed Neil. "Quiet, Sam! And that goes for you, too, Squirt!"

He tore himself away from the police drama he had been watching on television and followed his excitable Border collie and equally high-spirited little sister to the door.

A tall stranger stood in the glow of their security light. The dark shadows cast on his face by the powerful beam made it difficult for

1

Neil to see him properly. But it was light enough to see the large, hairy, brown dog sitting obediently at the man's side.

"Can I help you?" asked Neil. He shivered a little as a blast of cold air blew in from outside.

"Well, I hope so," said the stranger. "This is King Street Kennels?"

"Yes," replied Neil.

"I need to see someone about boarding my dog . . ."

"I'm afraid the kennels are closed now. We open again at eight tomorrow." Neil couldn't keep the edge of annoyance out of his voice. He hated it when people came at strange hours to leave their dogs. They seemed to have no idea about the way professional kennels were run.

"This is rather an emergency. Perhaps I could talk to your father?"

At that moment Bob Parker came up behind Neil.

"What's the problem?" he asked quietly.

Neil backed away from the door, but stayed near, his curiosity aroused, and absently rubbed Sam's ears. They both had a good view of the man's dog, which hadn't moved. It was some kind of crossbreed, thought Neil.

Definitely a touch of Airedale. Strangely, it showed no interest in Sam at all, and both man and dog seemed oblivious to the cold, damp October evening.

Neil shifted his gaze to the man again. He wore an expensive-looking grey raincoat and his shiny black hair was perfectly shaped, as if he had just come from the barber's. He reminded Neil of the clean-cut hero of one of the old-fashioned black and white movies they sometimes showed on daytime TV.

"I'd no idea they were going to spring this business trip on me," the man was saying. "Normally, my sister looks after her, but she's visiting friends in Manchester and I have to be at the airport at five-thirty in the morning. Anyway, even though the pups aren't due for another three weeks, my sister would have been nervous. A friend recommended King Street Kennels."

He gave them a hopeful look. "I'm prepared to pay double your fee if it will help you make up your mind . . ."

"That won't be necessary," Mr Parker replied briskly. "It is rather late, Mr Harding, but I can see that you're in a genuine fix. In view of the circumstances, of course we'll take

Jessie. I'll need a current vaccination certificate for her and a week's boarding fee in advance, if that's OK?"

Jessie. So that was the dog's name. While Mr Harding completed the formalities with his dad, Neil edged out of the door and squatted down. He held out his hand cautiously for her to sniff, and when Jessie's tail thumped on the ground to indicate her acceptance of him, he gently rubbed the dog's shaggy chest. She put out a long pink tongue to lick his hand.

Mr Harding looked down at them and smiled. "It looks as if my Jessie has made a new friend already," he observed, ruffling the wiry hair behind Jessie's ears.

"My son has a natural affinity with dogs, Mr Harding," said Bob Parker. "I can assure you that she will be in excellent hands here. And you don't have to worry about Jessie's condition. We've had bitches in whelp here before and we know what level of nutrition and exercise they need."

A relieved expression crossed Mr Harding's face. "Fine. Well, thanks again. I'm sure Jessie will be well cared for. I'll try to ring from Tokyo to see how she's doing, but it might be a little difficult, what with the time difference and the fact that I'll be tied up in meetings . . ." He bent down to give Jessie a final pat. "Bye, Jess. It's only for a week and then I'll be back. Be a good girl."

He handed her lead to Bob and turned, walking away briskly towards his mud-splashed white van without a backward glance. The grubbiness of the vehicle seemed at odds with the immaculate appearance of its driver. Neil stared as the brake lights glowed red. His eyes followed the van as it crackled down the gravel drive, then, with a shrug, he turned his attention back to their new guest.

Jessie stood, slowly wagging her huge, feathery tail and whining softly, as if willing her master to change his mind and come back for her.

Neil placed his hand on the dog's head to comfort her.

"Daddy, Daddy, that man was—" Sarah began.

"I've told you a dozen times that it's rude to stare at people, Sarah," said Mrs Parker, walking up the hallway towards them.

"But he had funny hair, Mummy!"

"Don't be silly, dear. Now, run upstairs. It's way past your bedtime!"

Sarah started her usual bedtime pouts and protests.

"Is it OK if I kennel Jessie?" asked Neil, anxious to escape from Sarah's whines.

"Yes, of course," his mother replied. "I'll come along to the office and write up her card."

King Street Kennels and rescue centre was situated behind the Parkers' house and garden. The fields and meadows which lay beyond were ideal for exercising the dogs. Compton town centre was a couple of miles away.

With Sam bounding alongside, Neil took Jessie's lead from his father and made his way across the yard with her to the kennels. Although she had ignored Sam when he had attempted to sniff her on the doorstep, Jessie now wagged her tail and pricked up her ears with interest as the Border collie came near.

"Make friends, Sam," Neil told him.

The two dogs sniffed each other and exchanged doggy greetings. It looked as though they would get on well together.

Sam began to bounce around, trying to interest Jessie in a game. "Sit!" commanded

Neil. Sam obeyed immediately but, to Neil's surprise, Jessie sat, too.

Neil decided to conduct an experiment. He knew he was taking a risk and that his parents would be furious if Jessie ran off, but he felt instinctively that she wouldn't. Letting go of her lead, he said, "Stay." Then he walked across the yard.

Sam quivered in his desire to follow Neil. His whole body was wriggling and his tail was banging the ground. In complete contrast to the Border collie, Jessie sat calmly, not moving at all, her bright brown eyes following Neil, her ears pricked for any order he might be about to give.

"Sam – come, Sam!" Before Neil had finished calling Sam's name for the first time, the dog was off, bounding up to his eleven-year-old master, his pink tongue lolling in a panting grin.

If Neil had expected Jessie to follow in his wake, he was wrong. She was still obeying his command to "stay".

"Jessie. Come now, Jessie." Neil clapped his hands and the brown dog with the shiny black nose trotted up to him.

"Good girl," Neil told her. He gave the new arrival a pat, glanced round to make sure he hadn't been spotted by his mother, and then picked up her lead again. Although it was evening, the yard was quite well lit. But he was in luck – no one had seen him.

They walked over to the kennel block where Jessie was to be housed for the week. Jessie walked perfectly to heel the whole time. Neil was amazed at how well trained she was. She didn't flinch when he opened the outside door to Kennel Block One with a clatter and switched on the lights. Even when a dozen or so dogs all started barking at once, her only reaction was to twitch her ears.

It was the half-term holiday and the kennels were almost full; Jessie was lucky to have secured the last space.

Neil took Jessie into her pen. He released her from her lead and hung it on a hook beside the mesh door. In the fluorescent light he could see that her hairy coat was mostly a deep golden colour, with hints of black along her back, on the tips of her ears and in her tail feathering. She had an alert, intelligent expression. While Neil went off to fetch a bowl of fresh water for her, Jessie ran round the pen, sniffing everywhere and investigating her neighbours on each side.

In the kennels office, Neil's mother, Carole, was busy completing the registration card for Jessie. It was important that detailed records were kept of every dog they boarded.

"Should I give Jessie any food tonight?" Neil asked her, putting his head round the open doorway.

"It's bit late, I think, Neil," she said, "but you might give her a biscuit bone, just in case she missed a meal. You'll need to get one from the store."

The store was situated between the two kennel blocks and it didn't take Neil long to find what he wanted.

On his way back, he couldn't pass any of the other dogs without having a quick word with each of them. One special favourite was a gentle German shepherd called King, who was a regular visitor because his owners often went abroad.

Most of their boarders settled in quickly. The Parkers gave them plenty of caring attention and exercise, and it was rare that they found a dog too difficult. Bob and Carole usually suggested that new dogs had a one-night stay first, to get them used to the kennels and prepare them for when their owners went away for a longer period.

Of course, it was a different story for the rescue centre. Often these dogs had been so badly treated or neglected that it took the Parkers some time to persuade them to trust human beings again.

Returning to Jessie's pen, Neil found her lying stretched out with her nose between her paws, looking dejected.

"Here you are, Jessie. Special treat for you!" He held out the biscuit to her.

Jessie stood up and came over to examine it. She sniffed and took it gently in her mouth, then dropped it on the floor and turned away.

"Don't you want it?" asked Neil.

She didn't seem the least bit interested, unlike Sam, who was fidgeting at Neil's side, licking his lips and eyeing the biscuit greedily. Jessie flopped down on the floor again, raised her shaggy eyebrows and gave a big sigh.

Perhaps the puppies were making her tired, Neil thought. "Don't worry, Jessie. It'll all seem better in the morning," he promised her cheerfully.

Neil switched off the lights and secured the door to the kennel block.

"Come, Sam," he called. "Time for bed!"

Neil awoke to the sound of his sister, Sarah, singing at the top of her voice. "Miss Polly had a dolly who was sick, sick, sick," she sang. "So she sent for the doctor to come quick, quick, quick." Then Neil heard her counting the stairs as she went down them. "One step, two steps, three steps, four . . ."

Neil groaned and pushed his head under

the pillow. Sarah was always much too lively in the mornings – not Neil's style at all.

Downstairs, Neil's parents were at the big, wooden kitchen table with his other sister, Emily, reading the local newspaper. They were talking about their plans for the day. King Street Kennels was a family business, and the whole family joined in when they could. Bob and Carole also employed a full-time kennel maid, Kate McGuire.

"We still haven't found a home for Sausage and Mash," said Emily, "so I think it's time the Puppy Patrol stepped in!" The Puppy Patrol was the name Neil's classmates at school had given them, because their whole lives revolved around dogs and the kennels.

"I have a suggestion to make." Emily gazed seriously at her parents to get their attention, but had to wait while Sarah settled herself noisily in her place.

Sausage and Mash were two small mongrel puppies in the rescue centre. They were about eight weeks old, and had been left for dead next to an old railway line. The Parkers hadn't found homes for either of them yet, so Emily had taken them on as her special project.

"Fine," murmured Mr Parker, buttering more toast. "Let's hear it, then."

"I think we should keep them!" Sarah chipped in, tipping too many cornflakes into her bowl so that some fell on the floor.

Fortunately, Sam was under the table ready to hoover up any crumbs.

"Careful, Sarah," said her mother, putting the cereal packet safely to one side. "You know we can't have any more pets. Sam and Fudge are quite enough for us."

Emily coughed loudly, annoyed at the interruption. "As I was saying," she continued, "my idea is that we should ring Mr Brooke and ask him to write about them in the *Compton News*."

Mr Brooke, the editor of the local newspaper, sometimes boarded his Great Dane at King Street Kennels and was always prepared to give the rescue centre a bit of publicity. A good story would sell more copies, too.

"Good idea, Em. I'll phone him after breakfast," said her dad.

"Can't I do it?" asked Emily.

Mr Parker smiled and glanced at his wife. He knew how important this was for Emily. "Yes, I suppose so. Ask to speak to Mr Brooke himself, though, and say you're from King Street Kennels."

Emily nodded and gulped down her breakfast with an excited smile on her face. She couldn't wait to get her pet project moving. Sausage and Mash were absolutely adorable. She felt sure that half of Compton would want to offer them homes, once their cute faces had appeared in the *News*.

Neil breezed into the kitchen then, pausing

long enough at the table to make himself a marmalade sandwich. "I'm just going to take a look at Jessie," he explained as he headed for the door, sandwich in hand.

"Neil! I'm going to ring the newspaper about Sausage and Mash!" Emily called after him.

"Hey, that's great, Em!" His voice floated back through the door but he had already disappeared, with Sam slipping away silently after him.

Mrs Parker sighed. "Mornings are like the bus station in this place," she complained. "Everybody zooming around, all going to different destinations."

It was true. But no matter what the rest of his family were up to, Neil's day always started with the dogs. They were the last thing he thought about each night when he fell asleep, and probably the first thing on his mind when he woke up.

As Neil walked across the courtyard towards the kennels he couldn't wait to see Jessie. There was something about that dog which made her stand out from the rest of their boarders. He couldn't put it into words, but it was something very special indeed, and he was determined to find out more about her.

Chapter Two

" . . . And so you see, if we don't find a home for them soon, I don't know what we're going to do." Emily's voice held just the right tremble of anxiety. Neil guessed it would be difficult for even a tough journalist and newspaper editor like Mr Brooke to resist.

"This morning? Yes, yes, that'll be fine. Thanks very much, Mr Brooke." Emily put the phone down and punched the air. "Yee-hah!" she yelled victoriously, her brown eyes shining. "Mr Brooke's going to send a photographer!"

There were cheers from the family.

"Well done, Emily," said her mum, laughing.

"Maybe you've got a career ahead of you as our Executive Publicity Officer."

Emily smoothed her dark brown hair. "We had to do something," she said. "Hardly anybody's been into the rescue centre lately."

"We never get many people during the school holidays," Neil reminded her. "They're all away. That's why we've got so many boarders."

"But school holidays can also be the time when people abandon their pets," said their dad, "rather than pay for kennels while they go on holiday."

Neil looked down at Sam, remembering how they had rescued him when *he* was a puppy. Some people could be unbelievably cruel to their animals, and it made him so angry.

"Well," said Carole Parker, sensing that they were all becoming a bit gloomy, "let's see what Emily's publicity does for Sausage and Mash. With any luck we can persuade the paper to give us another plug for the work we do at the centre and – who knows? – we could get trampled in the rush of people coming to offer good homes."

"Is anyone going to do any work today," said Emily, "or am I on my own? We need to get the place looking respectable for the photographer!"

"Yes, madam. Right away, madam!" Bob said, pretending to touch a non-existent cap. "Maybe you ought to be Head Foreman as well!"

Outside, the pale, clear sky and apricot rays of early sunshine promised a beautiful autumn day. The racket coming from the kennels told Neil that Kate McGuire, their kennel maid, was already at work. The boarders sounded excitable, anticipating their breakfast.

"Morning, Kate!" Neil called as he made his way down the line of pens.

"Hi, Neil." Kate strode towards him, grinning broadly, carrying a couple of food dishes. She was wearing jeans and a sweatshirt, and her long blonde hair was swept up in an untidy ponytail. "You helping out again today, then?"

Neil looked at his watch. "Yeah, later on, anyway. I'm taking Sam out first."

"Oh, who's this?" Kate stopped at Jessie's pen, putting the bowls on the floor so she could squat down to talk to her. "Hello, sweetheart. We haven't seen you before, have we?"

"This is Jessie." Neil told her all about Mr Harding and his after-hours visit the previous night. "Apparently she's expecting pups in three weeks' time," he informed Kate, who was stroking and admiring Jessie.

"Oh?" Kate peered closely at Jessie. "She doesn't look very pregnant, but bitches do carry their puppies quite high. They're tucked right up under the ribcage until the final week or so. Then the pups drop lower down and get ready to be born. With Jessie, though, it's hard to see where her tummy stops and her hair begins!"

Neil laughed. He took Jessie's lead off the hook, went into her pen and clipped it on to her collar. "I'd like to take her out with Sam," he said.

"Could you manage another two as well? We've got a lot to walk at the moment."

"OK. Any two?"

"How about Max and Flora, then you won't have too many big dogs to handle," said Kate mischievously.

"Since when was that a problem?" said Neil, indignant.

Kate grinned. "Just winding you up, Neil!"

Neil pretended to aim a kick at her ankle and Kate danced away with the bowls, laughing.

"I'll just get rid of these," she called back to him, "and then I'll come out with you."

Neil left Jessie clipped to the door of the kennel while he went to round up the other two dogs. They were regular boarders and he knew them well: Flora was a rough-coated Jack Russell with heaps of personality, while Max was a rather overweight dachshund who thought only of eating and sleeping. He could certainly do with some exercise.

Kate soon collected four of the other dogs and joined Neil outside the kennel block in the courtyard. The excited dogs took some controlling, but Kate quelled them all with a single *"Quiet!"*, delivered with so much authority that Neil fell silent for a few seconds, too.

With his three dogs trotting and padding beside him, Neil led the way to the gate leading out of the kennels enclosure. He whistled for Sam.

As he had expected, a streak of black and white shot out from under the hedge – Sam's favourite place – and raced them all to the gate.

"Hey, way to go, Sam!" said Kate as he passed her.

They caught up with Sam as he sat expectantly by the gatepost, wagging his tail. This was his chance to show off to the others.

"Open the gate, Sam!" Neil commanded.

Straight away, Sam leapt up at the latch and knocked it with his nose. The gate opened sufficiently for him to push his way through and make a gap wide enough for them all.

Neil praised and fussed the collie, then

waited for Kate and her team to come through before pulling the gate shut behind them.

"You ought to train him to shut it as well, you know!" Kate laughed.

They continued round the edge of the field. Flora was pulling ahead, impatient to be off, while Max, as usual, was lagging behind. Jessie was alert, but seemed content to keep pace with Neil. Sam, of course, ran freely, but came back frequently to circle round them all in sheepdog fashion and make sure they were keeping up.

Neil and Kate liked to let the dogs off the lead if they could, as they all enjoyed a free run. But it needed good judgement: few dogs were trained to Sam's level of obedience and once off the lead they could be uncontrollable. Flora, for instance, would disappear quickly down the first rabbit hole if she had the chance. Max, however, would flop down in the grass and wait for them to collect him on the way back.

Kate had brought two elderly golden retrievers, Prince and Alfie, together with a young Irish setter called Macduff. She would have to keep a firm hold of Macduff, because he had a tendency to take off like a rocket and not come back. Neil expected her to let the others have a good run about, though.

Walking briskly, Neil looked down at Jessie and wondered if he could trust her. She had been OK in the yard the previous night, but out in the fields was another matter entirely. Would she come back to him if he called her?

"Are you going to let Jessie have a run, Neil?" asked Kate, breaking into his thoughts.

"I was just wondering that," he said. "I'd like to try. She seems very well behaved."

Reaching the far side of the field, they all went through a second gate and began to climb up to the track that ran along the ridgeway. From there they would be able to see all over Compton and the surrounding countryside; patchwork fields, miniature farms and toy cows. It was a brilliant view.

Poor fat Max was finding the hill a trial, so Neil was obliged to slow down for him while Kate went on ahead. With Sam dancing round them with impatience, Neil thought this might be a good time to let Jessie have some freedom.

He bent to release Jessie's lead. "Now don't let me down, Jess," he said. "I'm counting on you being as good as Sam!"

Jessie looked up at him as if she understood. As soon as she was free, she ran over to Sam and they raced ahead together, chasing and sparring like playful pups. Neil laughed as he watched them charging down the hill. Suddenly he realized they were heading for the river.

"Oh, no!" he thought. His mum would shoot him if he let Sam get covered in mud! He sent out a piercing whistle.

"Sam! Jessie! Here! Come, Sam!" he yelled.

Both dogs stopped. Jessie looked back, uncertainly, but Sam hared back to Neil as if his life depended on it.

"Jessie!" Neil called again. "Come, Jess!"

This time she broke into an athletic lope, racing after Sam so that with her larger stride, she managed to arrive at Neil's feet at the same time as the collie.

"Good dogs!" Neil praised them, giving both a small titbit from the packet he always carried in his jacket pocket, and making plenty of fuss of them.

He looked enquiringly at Jessie. Who could have trained her that well? Harding had said he lived in Compton. King Street Kennels ran the only dog obedience classes in the district.

Jessie didn't look to be much more than two years old and, from the affection between her and Harding, Neil felt sure she had been with him since she was a pup. Either she was a natural wonder dog, or she had been to a very good class somewhere else, and if so, he wanted to know where.

As the brow of the hill appeared, Neil saw Kate sitting on a large stone with Macduff at her side and the other dogs wandering freely around them.

"Are you OK?" Kate asked him.

"Yeah, 'course. Did you see Jessie come back to me just then?"

"I did. You took a chance, though, didn't you? Suppose she hadn't come?"

Neil thought he had better not tell her about the previous night's experiment. "I just knew she would," he grinned. "I was more worried about them both diving into the river. I'd love to see what she's like at retrieving. I bet she's brilliant!"

"Come on, then," said Kate, getting up from her seat. "Let's find out." She called to her charges, who obediently trotted to her side and, with Sam leading, they went down a narrow footpath leading to a small knot of trees and bushes. Neil had often brought Sam here when he was training him: it was quiet, and away from distractions.

Once among the trees, Neil looped the leads of Max and Flora over a branch. Kate tied Macduff and the two retrievers next to them.

"You lot sit there for a while and watch," Neil said. "You might learn something!"

Max flopped down straight away, glad of the rest.

With Kate standing nearby, watching, Neil began to take Jessie through the routine of retrieving.

"Sit, Jessie!" he commanded. Jessie promptly sat on her haunches, watching him with interest. "Stay!"

Sam watched eagerly. He knew that a game was coming up. "Now, Sam, you're going to have to sit this one out," Neil told him. He ordered Sam to lie down and stay put. Then he looked about and found a good, stout stick.

"Here, Jessie. Have a good sniff of this." He showed it to Jessie, letting her sniff both the stick and his hands, then he turned and flung the stick as far as he could out of the copse. "Fetch, Jessie!"

The large brown dog took off after it. Her

pregnancy didn't appear to affect the speed at which she could run and in no time at all she had returned with the stick in her mouth. She ran up to Neil, sat down in front of him and waited, looking up at him with sparkling eyes.

"Give," said Neil. He tapped the side of his left leg.

Jessie immediately dropped the stick at his feet, then circled round him to sit closely at his side. It was as professional a performance as he had ever seen.

Kate laughed and clapped her hands, delighted.

"Atta girl, Jessie!" she cried. "That dog's got real showmanship, Neil!"

"Yep," Neil replied a bit absently. He was still puzzling over where Jessie had received such brilliant training.

He was just about to ask Kate if she knew of any other dog trainers in the Compton area, when Macduff suddenly tugged his lead free of the tree branch it had been tied to and ran off, yelping with excitement.

"Oh, no!" groaned Kate.

Stunned, she and Neil watched as the scatter-brained setter ran full tilt down the hillside, his lead flapping along beside him, grass and stones flying out in all directions.

"It'll take ages for us to catch him," Kate sighed. "He's definitely not a well-trained dog. If only it was Max, instead!"

"Kate!" gasped Neil, gripping her arm. "The fence!"

Macduff was charging towards an electrified sheep fence which stretched across the bottom end of the field.

"Here!" cried Kate, pushing the leads into Neil's hands. "I've got to stop him!" She sprinted after the dog as fast as she could.

Neil quickly gathered his wits in time to send Sam after her.

"Fetch them, Sam!" he commanded. "After them!"

The collie needed no persuading to veer away to the right, moving like lightning, as if to collect his straying sheep. Neil watched tensely.

Suddenly, a large, dark golden shape joined Kate as she ran, and quickly overtook her. It was Jessie. With powerful ease, she streaked after Macduff, purpose and discipline in each of her strides.

As Neil watched in disbelief, Jessie caught up with the runaway dog from behind and

took his lead in her mouth. She brought the setter to an abrupt halt just in front of the electric fence.

Meekly, and looking rather bemused, Macduff trotted beside her as Jessie tugged him back up the hill towards Kate and Neil. Sam ran back and forth behind them, making sure they were heading the right way.

"Neil, Neil!" gasped Kate when he caught her up. "Did you see that? What a great idea of yours, sending Jessie after Macduff. How did you know it would work?"

"It was nothing to do with me," Neil admitted. "Jessie did it all on her own. When I sent Sam, she went, too."

"Wow," said Kate, still breathless from her run. "I've never seen anything like it. Who did you say her owner was?"

"A man called Harding," Neil replied. "He lives in Compton but he's had to go to Japan on a business trip."

"If he lives in Compton, then who trained Jessie? I don't know of anybody else apart from us who trains dogs in such advanced stuff," said Kate. "I hope some rival hasn't started up classes . . ."

"Let's not say anything to my mum and dad about it," Neil said thoughtfully. "There's a mystery here and I want to be the one to solve it."

Chapter Three

As they neared the kennels, Neil glanced at his watch. They had been gone over an hour.

"Oh, no!" he groaned. "I'd forgotten all about the photographer coming. I promised Emily I'd help clear up."

Once the dogs were safely back in their pens, Neil went to join his sister in the rescue centre. Emily had done a good job of making the place look even cleaner and tidier than usual – by herself. Neil tried to hide his guilty feelings by whistling as he walked up to join the group already assembled there.

Emily gave him a quick scowl before she

turned back to the photographer, who was holding Mash and stroking him gently.

"You know, I'd take this little fellow home myself, if I could," he said, trying to keep a firm grip on the warm, wriggling puppy.

"Should I try to persuade you?" asked Mrs Parker as she came in behind Neil.

"No, it wouldn't be fair," the photographer said reluctantly, handing Mash back to Emily. "With this job, I'm hardly ever at home."

"Ah, what a pity," said Mrs Parker.

The photographer was a young man with long hair tied back in a ponytail. Neil had recognized him immediately. "You're the man who took the photos at the County Show this year, aren't you?"

The man nodded and smiled. "Jake Fielding." He shook hands with Neil and his mother. "Where's Sam?"

"Probably under the hedge, sleeping off his walk," Neil grinned. "I'll see if he'll come and say hello."

Neil walked back to the door and whistled. In no time, Sam came hurtling into the rescue centre and sat at Neil's feet, looking up at him expectantly.

Neil felt in his pocket for another treat.

The photographer knelt down to stroke him. "You're a beauty, Sam. I wish I had a dog like you."

Sam enjoyed all the fuss. He nosed in the photographer's pocket to see if he had any biscuits. Everybody laughed.

"Now then," the photographer said, getting to his feet once more. He took out a battered shorthand notebook. "Tell me all about Sausage and Mash here, and who's been looking after them. Great names, by the way."

Emily stepped forward. Now that her moment had arrived, she suddenly felt rather shy. She held a squirming brown and cream puppy in each hand while she gave Jake their story.

"Any idea what breed they might be?" Jake asked.

"Quite mixed, I'm afraid," said Mrs Parker. "Could be some boxer, and maybe some Staffordshire bull terrier. They're bound to be tough, smooth-coated, friendly, and with plenty of character, though!"

Jake laughed. "Well, you certainly know your dogs, Mrs Parker!"

"We see them all here," said Emily. "In fact,

pedigree dogs are just as likely to need rescuing as mongrels."

"Is that right?" said the photographer. "You'd think that if people spend a lot of money on a dog they'd be sure to look after it."

"Well, sometimes they grow bigger than people expect. And they have to be exercised every day," Emily told him. "Or they might need expensive medical treatment."

"What a rotten thing to do, abandoning your dog when it's ill and needs you most!" the photographer burst out.

Mrs Parker reached out and took one of the puppies from Emily. "My guess is that these arrived unexpectedly – maybe the mother was a pedigree Staffordshire and this litter was something of an embarrassment to her owner. In any event, they aren't valuable enough to sell for a decent price."

Jake studied the puppies thoughtfully. "Well, I think it's a real shame. Anyway . . ." he picked up his camera and quickly checked the light meter, "let's get a close-up of you, Emily, with a pup in each hand. Hold them near to your face, one either side. That's right. Lots of sentimental appeal to ooze off the page at our readers! Come on, puppies, give us a smile!"

Emily laughed and one of the pups licked her face just as the flash went off.

"Great! And again!"

Jake took lots of photographs from different angles. The puppies wriggled and squirmed, wanting to get down to play, while Emily beamed into the lens.

"There – that should do it," said Jake. He rewound the film and removed it from his camera. Quickly writing something on the label, he popped it into one of his many baggy pockets.

"By the way, I'd better ask which one's which," Jake said.

Neil took one of the pups from his sister.

"They look so alike, I'm not sure myself," he confessed.

"That's Mash!" Emily informed him crossly. "Surely you can tell by now? He's got three white paws and one brown one, and Sausage has got four white ones. If you spent as much time with them as *I* do, you'd—"

Just then Bob Parker called through the doorway and interrupted the row that was brewing.

"Neil! When you've finished up here, Kate would be glad of a hand," he said, and disappeared again.

"OK, Dad." He handed Mash back to Emily and then excused himself, saying that he looked forward to seeing Jake's story in the *News*.

Neil found Kate in Kennel Block One.

"We've got four dogs going home and four new ones arriving today," said Kate. "I'd be glad of some help with scrubbing out the pens."

Neil nodded. Not the best job in the kennels, he thought.

"Two pens each," said Kate. "I'll go into Block Two, and you can stay in here if you like. Oh, and you might take a look at our heroine. After all that running about, she seems to have flaked out. I haven't forgotten about what you said, by the way. I'll ask around, see if anyone's heard of another trainer. Did Harding say how long he'd lived in Compton?"

Neil shook his head. "No, just that he lived at 149 Dale End Road. I checked the address on his card in the office."

"Hmm." Kate pursed her lips, thinking hard, but said no more on the subject. She promised to try and see him later and check how clean he had managed to get the pens.

Jessie was sleeping, her head on her front paws. Unlike the other dogs, Jessie seemed a slow and dainty eater. Despite the energy she had used up earlier, she had only finished about half of her food.

Neil picked up a brush and started attacking the empty pen. He hoped she would be OK.

Jessie still hadn't eaten much food when it was time for the kennels to be closed up for the night. Neil was helping his mother with the routine locking-up and pointed it out.

"Should I take this away and give her some fresh?" he asked.

"I don't think there's much point," said Carole Parker. "She's obviously quite well. Some bitches eat a lot when they're expecting, and some go off their food. We have to let them tell us what they want. Maybe we should let Jessie take it easy tomorrow. Just a stroll around the yard, not a marathon trek like the one you took her on today."

"Fine. I was planning to go over to Chris's tomorrow anyway, so it suits me not to have to take any of them for a long walk." Chris Wilson was Neil's best friend from school. "He's going to show me his new bike. Wish *I* had a new one, Mum . . ."

"You'd better start thinking of ways to earn one, then." Carole Parker glanced around the courtyard. "The kennels will be due for a new coat of paint soon."

"Oh, Mum!" Neil groaned. His old bike, which was feeling slightly small for him these days, would just have to last a while longer.

Chapter Four

Tuesday was a rainy day and nobody was in a good temper. Even the dogs seemed miserable. Sam was sprawled on the doormat with his head on his paws. He looked as if he wanted to go for a walk, but every time the door was opened, he shrank back, tail between his legs, as a flurry of rain blew in.

The kennels were a dismal place to be. Despite having playthings, comfortable quarters and plenty to eat, every dog seemed to be moping and scowling. Neil and Emily's attempts to get Max the dachshund out for a walk had failed. He had simply splayed out his paws and, after having dragged him a few inches with his claws rasping on the floor of his pen, they had given up and let that particular sleeping dog lie.

Neil was in his bedroom, idly flicking through a football magazine but not really reading it.

"What's up with you, then?" said Emily, breezing in and plonking herself down at the end of his bed with a bounce.

"I keep thinking about Jessie. I can't get her off my mind."

"That brown dog who rescued Macduff?"

"Yes," said Neil. "*That* brown dog. I think she's the most intelligent, talented dog we've ever had here, you know. She's only stopping for a week, but I want to find out everything she can do."

"Isn't she having puppies?" Emily said. "Do you think she'll have them while she's with us?"

"I'm afraid not. She's not due for another two and half weeks and Mr Harding's picking her up on Friday."

"That man!" Emily's lips pursed.

"What do you mean?"

"I think I agree with Sarah that he's weird."

"Sarah can't have said that," Neil pointed out.

"No. 'Funny' is what she said."

"Anyway, what do you know? I saw him and he was perfectly normal. There was a real bond between him and Jessie. *You* didn't even see him," Neil reminded her. "You were glued to the box!"

Emily shrugged and nodded. "I've still got this . . . *feeling* about him, though," she said.

"You can't believe Sarah – she's only a baby!" scoffed Neil.

"Let's see this wonderful Jessie of yours," said Emily, changing the subject before they started arguing. It seemed everybody was arguing with everybody else today. In the house, their parents were fighting over what colour to paint the kennels. Carole Parker favoured green, while Bob said that white was more hygienic and clean looking. Sarah was in her most demanding mode, requiring everybody to find things for her. So Emily had been glad of a chance to slip out to the kennels with her brother.

They came to Jessie's pen. She immediately sat up and thumped her tail.

"Looks like she fancies a walk," Emily observed.

"You could be right. Let's just take her as

far as the field, though. I don't want to wear her out. Or me." Neil said.

Sam appeared as they clipped Jessie's lead on, and waited to be allowed to open the gate. Once in the field, Neil let Jessie off her lead. He demonstrated her skills at sitting and staying and Emily threw a ball for her to retrieve.

"This is really easy for her," he said. "She's capable of far more."

His sister had a sudden idea. "I wonder if she can understand left from right?"

"You try," Neil suggested.

Emily threw the ball for Jessie, then asked her to stay. She obeyed. Then Emily yelled, "Right, Jessie. Go right", while gesturing with her right hand.

To their amazement, Jessie loped off to the right-hand hedge, where she stopped and looked questioningly at them.

"OK, Jessie. Left, left!" Emily shouted, this time pointing with her left hand. Jessie trotted over to the opposite hedge, then sank down, waiting for her next instruction.

Emily's face was animated. "This is incredible! Look what I'm going to try now," she said. "Round, Jessie. Round in a circle!"

She drew a circle in the air with her fingers. Jessie hesitated for a moment, as if this was something she dimly remembered but hadn't done for ages, then she trotted round in a tight, neat circle and sat down again.

Emily ran over to her and gave her a pat and a stroke. "Good girl. Clever girl!" she praised her and gave her a doggy treat from Neil's packet. "She must have had a really good trainer, Neil. Don't you think?" Emily commented.

Neil raised his eyebrows and grunted. He and Kate were already on this particular case, and what he had just seen Jessie do made him even more determined to crack it.

The following morning, the trees and grass sparkled with raindrops but the rain had stopped. Neil had promised Chris that they would go for a long bike ride if it was dry. Before he set off, Neil made his usual breakfast visit to see how the dogs were getting on.

Fat Max was going home that day. "I'm going to give his owners a diet sheet. It's disgusting, letting a dog get into that state," Kate said.

"You wait till you see them," Neil chuckled. "I was here when they brought him in. Ever heard that owners look like their pets?"

Neil gave Max a scratch on his big fat belly. He peered into Jessie's pen opposite and sighed. The dog was sleeping and looked very peaceful.

"By the way, I made some enquiries yesterday," Kate told him. "About Harding. I rang up all my doggy friends and, apart from that place over at Stackbridge – you know, the place run by that awful woman who breeds chihuahuas – nobody knows of anyone running training and obedience classes within twenty miles. That's why they all come here."

Neil frowned. "So Jessie must have been trained somewhere other than Compton," he said. "I wonder how long Mr Harding has been living here?"

"Never, by the look of things," Kate said. She smiled triumphantly.

"What on earth do you mean?"

"My friend Jane lives in Dale End Road – at number 139. The last house is number 147. Harding told us he lived at 149. Well, that house doesn't even exist!"

"Phew, this is tough going, isn't it?" Neil complained, wiping the back of his hand across his brow as he and Chris halted their bikes. They were halfway to the ridge.

They had started off by following the route Neil and Kate had taken with the dogs two days earlier. Then, in order to give Chris's new bike the proper test that he wanted, they had left the track and plunged into the patch of woodland that grew thickly on one side. Neil, with his older, narrower tyres and fewer gears, puffed in Chris's wake. Whereas Chris's bike bounded over tree roots and tufts of grass, Neil's kept lurching to a halt, almost hurling him over the handlebars more than once.

Despite the weather and the fact that it was a half-term holiday, they hadn't seen one other cyclist or walker on this particular part of the hill.

"Shh." Chris held up his hand as Neil opened his mouth to say something. "Listen . . ."

"To what?"

"The silence."

"You can't listen to silence, dummy. You can only listen to sounds."

"What's that?"

Both boys held their breath, tense with concentration.

"I can't hear a thing," Neil said.

"Shh!" ordered Chris.

After what seemed like an endless wait, Neil grew fed up. "It was a blackbird," he snorted.

"I didn't mean the bird. There was definitely something else. It was a sort of whimpering sound, like an animal in pain," insisted Chris.

"There are plenty of foxes around here," Neil pointed out.

"It didn't sound like a fox. Maybe something's fallen and hurt itself. Perhaps we should have a look around," said Chris.

"OK, but not for too much longer. We've got a big food delivery arriving and I promised Mum I'd be back by one."

They dragged and bounced their bikes over roots and stones, across ditches and under branches, but failed to see or hear anything out of the ordinary. In the end, they had to head for home.

Chris didn't come all the way with Neil. After coming through the field, he stopped by the first gate. "I think my gears need seeing to. I'm going to take them apart here. You go on," he said. "See you."

"Yeah. Tomorrow?"

"OK," Chris agreed.

The two of them met again much sooner than they had intended. It was about ten past three that afternoon and Neil was helping to unload boxes of dog food from the delivery van and put them away in the food store, when he heard Chris call his name. There was something strange about his voice – an urgency – that told him instantly that something was wrong.

Telling his dad that he'd be back in a moment, he raced over to the main gate, where Chris was waiting for him. Instead of sitting astride his bike, Chris was standing beside it and his right arm was stretched across something that was balanced awkwardly between the crossbar and the saddle.

As Neil drew nearer, he could see that a makeshift stretcher, constructed from branches, had been lashed together with Chris's belt and the cable from his cycle lock. On it lay a dark, still shape.

A cold, creepy sensation washed over Neil. He felt slightly sick. "What is it?" he called over his friend.

"A dog. He's in a very bad way."

Chapter Five

"Dad. *Dad!*" yelled Neil. "Come here, quick!"

Gently, they lifted the heavy, unconscious animal down from the bike. Then Chris leant the bike against the fence and attempted to rub some life back into his numb arm. He had been carefully holding the home-made stretcher in position for almost half an hour.

"Where did you find him?" Neil asked, watching as his father quickly assessed the situation and took the dog into the treatment room.

"I was back up on the ridge. I heard the sound again and managed to get a fix on it. I found him lying in a shallow stream. I think he'd tried to get a drink and collapsed."

"Let's go and see how he is."

The dog was lying on the examination table. From the shape of his ears and muzzle, and the deep brown and black colour of his coat, he looked, to Neil's experienced eyes, to be some kind of Dobermann cross.

Bob Parker was on the phone to the vet. "Bad wound to his back leg, Mike," he was saying. "And one of his eyes is badly swollen. It looks as if he's been hit by something."

Mike Turner was an old friend of the Parkers and a frequent visitor. He said he would come over right away.

The injured dog stirred. He made a feeble effort to lift his head. It looked almost too heavy for his neck to support.

"You don't think he's broken any bones in his neck or back, do you?" Neil asked his father.

"Don't think so. He wouldn't be able to move his head at all if that was the case."

Bob Parker placed a tin bowl of water in front of the dog. He appeared to want it, but didn't have the strength to lap, so Neil fetched a dropper and dripped some water into the dog's mouth.

"Shouldn't you give him some food as well? He might be starving to death!" asked Chris.

"Not until the vet has seen him. We don't know what this chap has been through. He might have internal injuries," Bob said.

Neil put a blanket over the dog, who was shivering.

When Mike Turner arrived, he gave the dog an expert examination and announced that it had multiple abrasions and four broken ribs.

"It looks as if he might have been kicked or beaten," he said grimly. "They're new injuries. You can tell by the colour of the bruise round his eye. It can't be more than twenty-four hours old. It's this wound on his leg that's done most of the damage, though. See here?"

Mike parted the blood-matted fur. They saw the deep gouge carved in the animal's back leg. "I can't tell what has caused it. It's not a knife wound – wrong shape. But it's shattered the bone just here, and nicked a vein. He's probably lost quite a lot of blood."

"Lying in the water won't have helped," said Neil.

"No. He may be suffering from hypothermia. The water will have been freezing." The vet turned to Chris. "Where exactly was the spot where you found him?"

"In the woods near the ridge."

"Well, you do get poachers going up there, shooting wood pigeon and rabbits. It could be a bullet wound, I suppose," Mike said. "That would have caused this clean, deep cut. But I don't know how he could have sustained the other injuries, unless he was mistreated."

Mike stopped and frowned. He looked at the dog on the table again. "No, he's quite well fed and looks as if he was in good shape until this happened."

"I wonder why nobody's reported him missing?" said Chris.

"I don't know," said Mr Parker. "We'll report all this to the police, of course."

"You do that, Bob," said Mike. "Meanwhile, I'm going to take him to the intensive care unit and see what I can do for him."

"Will he be OK?" asked Neil.

Mike shrugged. "It's touch and go. He's in shock. The sudden blood loss hasn't done him any favours, either."

"We know you'll do your best, Mike," said Mr Parker. "Keep us updated, won't you?"

"Sure thing," Mike promised. "Give him twenty-four hours, and then you can come and see him." He paused and added, "We'll need a name for him."

"I think we should call him Soldier," said Chris, "because he's been so brave."

There was no disagreement.

"OK. Soldier it is."

After Mike Turner had left, Bob Parker turned to Neil and Chris. "The best thing you two can do now is get stuck into some work. No sense in worrying too much about Soldier – Mike will let us know soon enough if he's going to make it or not."

Neil nodded, but he was still upset.

"I'd better be off home," announced Chris, looking at his watch.

Neil walked him to the front gate.

"You OK, mate?" asked Neil, sensing his friend was still a bit knocked sideways by the afternoon's events.

"Just about. Will you let me know if you hear any more from the vet, or if you find his owner?"

"You'll be the first to know," Neil promised.

"I think I might go up there again. See if I can find any cartridge shells."

"Mind you don't get hit yourself," said Neil.

"Poachers usually operate at night. I'll be all right. Anyway, I'm a bit bigger than a pigeon or a dog. They couldn't miss me."

"That's just what I'm worried about!" said Neil. Then his voice was serious again. "I'll go to the vet's tomorrow. You coming?"

"You bet!" said Chris.

The mood in King Street Kennels next morning was sombre. Everyone had heard about Soldier and although work went on as normal, there was a tense atmosphere of expectancy as they waited to hear from Mike Turner.

54

Chris was at the back door just as Neil was finishing his breakfast. "Any news about Soldier yet?"

"No, nothing – it's a bit early, though," Neil told him. "I'm just going to check on Jessie. Want to come?"

"Can I come too?" Sarah squeaked excitedly.

"Oh, do take her with you," Carole begged them. "I've got loads to do and she's really bugging me this morning."

"OK," Neil agreed, reluctantly. Why did he have to put up with a kid sister hanging around? Chris was grinning at him, enjoying Neil's frustration.

Kate was out with some of the dogs when they got to the kennel block. They found Jessie lying in a corner of her pen, looking rather bored.

"Can I stroke her?" Sarah asked them.

"Of course you can," said Neil, opening the pen.

The big, gentle dog thumped her tail as Sarah stroked her head very gently.

"What's this?" Chris enquired, pointing to a piece of folded paper poked through the wire of Jessie's pen.

Neil pulled it out. It was from Kate, addressed to him.

He read it aloud: *I think Sam's feeling a bit neglected. Why don't you give him some training exercises today?*

"Can I come and watch?" begged an eager voice from Jessie's pen. "*Please*. I won't get in the way! I promise!"

"But you always do—" Neil began.

"She'll be OK," said Chris. "I can keep an eye on her while you work the dogs."

Neil raised his eyes in mock despair. "It's a conspiracy! Come on then. We'll take Jessie, too."

While Sarah sat on a bench, stroking the two dogs, Neil and Chris struggled out onto the field, carrying old tyres, planks, a barrel and some balls. They made several journeys before Neil was satisfied. "This should do," he said at last.

Sam was getting very excited, fidgeting in his place. Even Jessie had her ears pricked up with interest.

Neil and Chris then built the runs, put up posts for the dogs to weave through, erected planks for them to run along, tyres to squeeze through, and a length of wood balanced over some bricks to make a see-saw.

Once it was finished, Chris flopped onto the bench next to Sarah, wiping his brow.

Neil called Sam. Immediately, he rose from his place beside Sarah and came over to him.

"Good boy!" Neil said. He looked over at Jessie. "And let's see what you make of all this, Jess."

Neil led Sam to the start of the Agility course. He could sense Jessie watching them expectantly, all her senses alert. She made a move to follow Sam.

"No, Jess. You can't do it," he said. "We don't want you to fall off anything. You might hurt your puppies."

Jessie's reaction was a sharp, impatient bark and a whine, as if she were saying, "Go on, let me."

Neil remembered his mother saying that pregnant bitches knew how much food and exercise they wanted, and you had to let them tell you. Jessie was a sensible, intelligent dog. She wouldn't put her puppies at risk. If there was a jump or an activity she wasn't capable of doing, she simply wouldn't do it.

"OK – go, Jess, go!" he commanded, and held on to Sam's collar as a precaution.

To Neil's delighted surprise, Jessie bounded over and leapt onto the first plank. Then she ran swiftly, negotiating each obstacle as if she'd been doing it all her life. She flew through the tyres without hesitating, and only slowed down for the rather wobbly see-saw. She completed the course quickly and without a fault, finishing with a tidy return to sit at Neil's feet.

"That's incredible," said Chris. "She must have done it before, surely?"

"This dog gets more amazing by the minute," Neil replied, grinning proudly as he rubbed her head.

"Now it's Sam's turn," Chris said.

Neil was idly looking round the exercise field. "Hang on. Where's Sarah?"

Chris looked round, too. There was no sign of her.

"She can't have gone far." Chris felt rather uneasy. He had promised to keep an eye on Sarah, but he'd been busy watching Jessie's performance. "Come on," said Chris. "Let's go and find her. I expect she's playing hide-and-seek."

"Wait, maybe Sam can show us where she is," said Neil. "Look, there's Sarah's hanky." He picked up the scrap of material from the bench and then held Sam still while he wrapped it loosely round the dog's nose. "Fetch, Sam. Fetch Sarah."

Sam bounded around Neil, barking excitedly. But his eyes were watching the hanky, to see if Neil was going to throw it for him.

"It's no good," said Neil. "He's not been trained to track people. He doesn't know what I want."

They called Sarah's name loudly, but she didn't appear.

"How about Jessie?" Chris suggested.

Neil looked down at the shaggy dog sitting patiently at his side. You never know, he thought. She might just be trained to do this, too.

"OK," said Neil, "We'll give it a try. You'll have to keep hold of Sam for me, Chris."

Neil draped Sarah's handkerchief over Jessie's nose.

Jessie sniffed it with interest.

"Find Sarah, Jessie. Where's Sarah? Find her!"

Jessie looked up at Neil once, then bounded away with her graceful lope. She seemed to know exactly where she was going, her nose down near the ground as she ran following the scent trail left by Neil's sister.

The boys ran behind, restraining Sam who was keen to join in this new game, and trying hard to keep Jessie in sight. She disappeared into a thick clump of trees and bushes at the far end of the field, and they heard her bark once.

Sam barked in reply, eager to follow.

Neil and Chris scratched and scraped their way through a tunnel of brambles. There, in the centre of her new den, they found Sarah, sitting on a moss-covered tree root with her arm round Jessie, grinning delightedly. Sam barged in, too, and started licking her face.

"Oh, Sam, stop!" she cried.

"Sarah, how could you run off like that? You frightened us to death!" said Neil. "We had to ask Jessie to find you."

Sarah gave a giggle. "I like playing hide-and-seek," she said. "Can we play it again?

"No, we definitely can't!" said Neil, angrily. "Come on, you're going back to the house."

"Jessie was pretty fantastic, Neil," said

Chris, brushing himself down once they were all out in the open field again. "Shouldn't you give her a biscuit, or something?"

Jessie's head cocked to one side and her tail began to wag.

Neil smiled in spite of being so mad about Sarah's game.

"Here, Jess!" he called.

Jessie needed no second prompting. She ran over to Neil's feet, sat rigidly and watched his every move as he put his hand into his pocket.

"Good girl, Jess. You were wonderful!"

"Look at Sam!" squealed Sarah.

Sam was sitting up on his haunches, waving both front paws in the air at Neil and making pathetic little whines.

"Crikey, Sam," said Neil. "When did you learn that little number?"

"I think he just taught himself!" gasped Chris, chuckling with laughter.

"Jessie's done it again though, hasn't she?" said Neil.

"Done what?"

"Something totally unexpected. She keeps showing off different bits of her training. If she were a different breed, I'd say she'd been trained as a police dog."

"Hey, you don't think Harding's really a policeman, do you?" said Chris.

"I'll have to ask him when he comes to pick her up. You know, you could have something there. If he were a detective working on a big case, he might not want anyone to know his real address." Neil had told Chris about the phantom 149 Dale End Road.

"Yes, but surely a policeman would know we might have to check out his address? It doesn't make sense . . ."

"No, it doesn't," Neil agreed. "C'mon, let's put all the stuff back in the store and get Sarah back inside. There might be some news about Soldier."

Chapter Six

They returned to the house to find everybody crowded around the big wooden table in the Parkers' kitchen. Bob had just got back from town with an early edition of the *Compton News* and a bag of doughnuts.

The paper was spread out on the table, surrounded by mugs of hot tea.

Sarah scrambled up on a chair to get a better view.

The headline leapt out from a corner of the third page. Underneath the banner was the photograph of Emily, with the puppies each side of her face staring appealingly into the camera. It was perfect.

"*SAUSAGE AND MASH IN DESPERATE BID TO FIND HOME,*" read out Bob Parker.

Emily's face was pink with pleasure. "It's good, isn't it?" she said.

"Terrific," said her father.

"Brilliant," her mother agreed. "We must ask them for a copy of that picture."

"Not bad, Em. But don't give up the day job," said Neil.

Emily dug him in the ribs with her elbow.

"What does the story say?" asked Chris, leaning over Mr Parker's back and trying to read. It was rather difficult with everyone moving the paper so that they could get a better look.

Bob Parker read the article out loud.

"*Could you abandon two little puppies like this? Well, somebody did! Sausage and Mash, seen here with nine-year-old Emily Parker, were found abandoned, cold and almost starved to death, near the old railway line in Compton. Now they desperately need homes. If you can help, ring King Street Kennels rescue centre. And they've put our number in.*"

"Well, if that doesn't generate some interest, I don't know what will," said Carole Parker.

Bob closed the newspaper. "Better stand back, Em, or you'll be flattened in the rush."

"Look, Bob, there's been another antiques robbery, in one of those big houses in Aston this time," Carole said, indicating the main headline. "Wasn't a shop in Leigh robbed, too?"

"It's the first I've heard about it," said Neil.

"Where have you been, Neil?" said Mrs Parker. "The last few months have been full of stories about thefts from homes and antique shops. The police reckon it's one gang, possibly organized by a mastermind."

"Making it the biggest crime wave around here for years!" Chris chipped in, knowledgeably.

Neil was surprised. "Why are you so interested?"

"My dad's friend had his shop in Padsham turned over last month," said Chris. "They took all the really good stuff. Worth about a hundred grand."

"A hundred thousand pounds?" Neil was stunned. "If they took that much every time, they must be making a fortune."

Just then the phone went. Mrs Parker answered.

"It's someone wanting to come and see Sausage and Mash," she said as she put the phone down.

"The first call of many, I should think," said Bob Parker. "We'd better get ready for the deluge."

"Has Soldier's owner reported him missing yet?" Neil asked his dad.

"I spoke to Sergeant Moorhead this morning. They've checked the missing dog lists but nobody's lost one resembling Soldier."

"It's very strange. He was well fed, so he couldn't be a stray. Do you think he could have belonged to a poacher and they don't want to claim him in case the police find out about them?"

"It's possible."

"Some rotten person might have chucked him out of a car. People do that sometimes, don't they?" said Emily.

The phone rang again.

"I think we'll find homes for those two bundles of mischief in no time!" said Mr Parker.

"I know!" said Emily, excitedly. "Why don't we get the paper to do an article on Soldier?

Then we might find out who owns him."

"Worth a try, Em," said her dad. Then his face clouded over. "But I think we'd better wait and see if he recovers first."

Leaving Mrs Parker and Emily to cope with the phone calls, Mr Parker and Neil went off to check on the dogs. Chris mounted his bike, waved goodbye and headed home.

"How's Jessie today?" Mr Parker asked.

"If you'd seen the way she went round Sam's obstacle course, you wouldn't need to ask," Neil said proudly.

Realizing he might have dropped himself in it, Neil quickly changed the subject. Boarders, particularly pregnant ones, weren't supposed to risk life and limb on Sam's training course. "I think she's missing her owner, though. She gets a bit depressed and whimpery some-times. Have you heard from him?"

"No, but there's a ten-hour time difference between here and Japan. It's probably very difficult for him to ring. He's due back tomorrow, anyway. And we don't need to worry about her puppies – they're not due yet. Puppies are never more than three days early or late, unless there's something wrong."

Emily came running up from the direction of the house.

"I had to find you," she said breathlessly. "Guess what? We've got fourteen people wanting to come and see the puppies!"

"Fourteen? That's fantastic!"

"But we've only got two puppies!" Emily looked anxious.

"I wouldn't panic," said Mr Parker reassuringly. "Not everyone's going to be suitable. We probably won't need to see them all."

"I just hope we don't choose whoever had Soldier."

Neil gazed at his sister. The possibility of Soldier's owners coming to claim one of Emily's two homeless puppies had never occurred to him.

There were only two people left in the vet's waiting room in Compton when Neil and Chris arrived that evening. Janice, the nurse, said they could go straight through to the Intensive Care unit and see Soldier. She warned them to be very quiet though, so as not to excite the other animals too much.

The IC section was a part of the surgery

that Neil and Chris had never seen before. The place was spotless, with gleaming shelves, glass-covered cabinets and shining emergency equipment. The patients here, though, were in individual cages, lying on sheepskin or special heated mats.

They would have missed Soldier if Janice hadn't pointed him out to them. With his injured leg shaved and splinted and a drip feed taped to his left foreleg, he looked utterly helpless. A small label at the top of the cage identified him and gave details about his date of admission and treatment.

"He's still very weak," Janice told them. "We've done all we can for him, but he's definitely got a touch of pneumonia, too."

"That sounds bad," said Neil worriedly.

"It's not good. Normally we'd expect antibiotics to clear it up, but after the shock and the loss of so much blood, he may not be strong enough to survive the infection." She paused. "Only time will tell."

After a few minutes of staring at Soldier and willing him to get better, they left the surgery, thanking Janice for her help, and mounted their bikes to cycle home in the gathering gloom of the autumn evening.

On their way, they stopped outside the window of the video shop, which was having a sale.

"I've been thinking," Neil said as they gazed at the display. "You know our theory about Mr Harding being an undercover policeman? You don't think he could be trying to find the antiques robbers, do you?"

Chris looked thoughtful. Then he said, "No, he can't be. Why put Jessie in the kennels for exactly a week? How would he know that it would take only a week to catch them? It doesn't make sense. Anyway, I've been thinking, too. If he's only just moved here, he could have got mixed up with Dale End Drive, round the corner. That goes up to 161 – I checked."

"I suppose so," said Neil. "You're probably right."

"By the way," Chris said, "I was up in the woods again today. I didn't find anything, though."

"Soldier might have run quite a long way from where he was injured. He must have been so scared. He probably just bolted."

"But there must be something we could do. Hey, what's going on?"

Neil spun round and saw a van careering erratically down the street towards them.

"The driver must be drunk!" said Chris.

The van was being hauled from one side of the road to another, but it looked too deliberate for the vehicle to be out of control.

"There's a car chasing it. Look!"

Neil spotted the black BMW which Chris had seen first. It was close behind the van.

"Quick! Get in the doorway!" Neil shouted urgently as the van headed in their direction.

They leapt into the shop doorway just in time. The van, with what looked like a ginger-haired driver at the wheel, mounted the pavement right where they had been standing, just missed a lamp-post, then shot off down a side street.

"He's going to kill somebody!" Chris said.

The BMW couldn't make the quick right-hand turn. It missed the entrance to the narrow lane and carried on down the road. Neil felt sure he'd seen three men in it – two in the front and one in the back.

Shaken, Neil and Chris stepped out of the doorway.

"Are you OK?" Chris asked.

"Just about. I wish I'd got their numbers so that we could have reported them. What do you think was going on?"

"I don't know. It looked as if the BMW was chasing the van and the van driver was trying to shake it off."

"Well, it worked. He got rid of them, didn't he?" Neil said.

"But why was the car chasing the van?" Chris wondered.

Neil shrugged. "Maybe it was Compton's first example of road rage. Perhaps the van carved up the BMW at the traffic lights."

"It looked a bit more serious than that to

me," Chris said. "That van driver looked as if he was scared for his life!"

"Maybe he'd done something dreadful, like robbing a bank—"

"Perhaps he owed money to the guys in the BMW—"

"Maybe it was a drugs thing . . ."

Their speculations ground to a halt, though the imaginations of both boys were working overtime as they slowly rode home.

Chapter Seven

Neil had meant to tell his parents about the car chase, but other events soon put it out of his mind.

"Whose car is in the drive, Mum?"

Neil threw his jacket on the banister and he and Chris joined Mrs Parker in the kitchen.

"Honestly, Neil, you wouldn't believe how many people have been in to see Sausage and Mash." Carole Parker looked harassed as she sorted through some papers on the table.

"That's great! Wish we'd got back earlier. I might have been able to help out," said Neil.

"I had to leave your father and Emily sorting them all out. If it was up to Emily, though, I don't think we'd ever find any homes for them!

She has doubts about everyone. She keeps thinking about Soldier, I suppose. How is he?"

"In a bad way. I could do some real damage to the person who did this to him!" Neil's threat was tinged with anger.

"This lot seem really nice." Carole tried to counter his high emotions with some good news. "It's going to be hard to choose between them, but I think Emily has settled on someone just now. It's their car outside."

Crossing to the rescue centre, Neil and Chris found Mr Parker and Emily saying goodbye to a girl and a boy, both aged about ten, and their parents. The younger girl was carefully carrying a wriggling Mash.

"Have both puppies gone now?" Neil asked his sister as the family drove away.

"Yes," said Emily, quietly. "It's awful. I miss them already. Dad's told them he'll be along in a week's time to make sure everything's OK."

"Well, at least you got what you wanted, Em. Good homes for them both," said her dad. "That's what we're all about."

"Do you always do that?" asked Chris. "Check up, I mean."

"Oh, yes," Mr Parker replied. "You have to make sure that the dog is happy and the new owners aren't having second thoughts. If there are any doubts at all, we'd rather bring the dog back." He turned to Neil. "Have you looked in on Jessie today?"

"Not yet. I haven't had a chance. Heard from Mr Harding yet?"

"Nope. I'm sure he'll ring as soon as he's home, though. He must be missing her by now. You saw the bond between them."

"Mm-hmm," agreed Neil.

"He might be wrong about when those pups are due, though. Her tum looks quite bulgy today. That doesn't normally happen till the eighth week. As you know, pregnancies are about nine weeks in all – sixty-three days."

"He'll be taking her home just in time, then."

"Looks like it."

At that moment, Neil's mother came running out of the office towards them, a stricken look on her face. "Mike Turner's just rung. He says Soldier isn't going to last the day out."

"Oh, no!" Chris let out a cry.

"I thought you might want Dad to take you back down there."

Neil and Chris exchanged glances and ran

towards the house. Emily looked at her mother then ran after them.

"It's the pneumonia, I'm afraid," Mike Turner explained when they arrived at the surgery. "We've done all we can but he's too weak to fight it. Poor chap."

"He's not got long left, then?" asked Neil.

"No. 'Fraid not. I'll leave you with him. I'll be in the office with your dad."

As they pushed through the double doors into the surgery, they could see Soldier lying in his special cage. The dog's shallow, fast, rasping breaths were painful to hear.

"Oh, Neil . . ." Emily didn't know what to say.

Neil put his arm round his sister's shoulders and gave her a comforting hug.

Chris stroked Soldier's silky head. "I was hoping I'd saved you," he said. "I wish I had . . ."

At that moment, as if responding to Chris's words, Soldier's hide rippled and he gave a little sigh. Then suddenly, the rasping breaths ceased.

Emily went white. She gaped at Neil, her hand to her mouth.

Neil shouted for the vet.

Mike pushed through into the IC unit moments later.

He moved up to the table and began feeling the dog with his hands. He lifted Soldier's head up very gently and looked into the dog's eyes. With a sigh he laid Soldier's head back down and pulled out the drip.

"He's gone, I'm afraid. There's nothing I can do now. I'm sorry." He looked at Neil, standing next to him. "Find me when you're ready. I'll be outside."

Neil felt gutted. He had never seen a dog die before. He'd had a pet dog before Sam, called Goldie, and he'd had to be put down. But Neil was so young then, and hadn't been around when it had happened.

Neil felt furiously angry. It was so frustrating, not knowing who this dog had belonged to or why he had been so badly treated. *Somebody* was responsible for Soldier's death and, even though he couldn't do anything to bring him back, Neil was determined to find out who was to blame.

Mike Turner had a small pets' cemetery in the surgery garden.

"If you like, we could bury Soldier there," he said. "We've not found the owner and the poor chap will need a proper send-off."

Neil and his father discussed it with the rest of the family and they all agreed that it was the right thing to do.

Bob and Mike dug a grave beside a pear tree in one corner of the small garden.

Sarah had done a drawing of Soldier with wings and a lop-sided halo – "So that he can go straight up to Heaven," she announced. She gave it to her father so that it could be put into the grave with Soldier.

The dog's body, wrapped in a white cloth, was lowered gently into the hole in the ground.

Neil had intended to make a speech, but in the end he felt he couldn't. Chris volunteered himself.

"We are here today to honour the Unknown Soldier," he said, standing over the shallow grave. "Though wounded in battle, he fought bravely to the last. Goodbye, Soldier."

"Goodbye, Soldier," they all muttered.

There was silence while Mike solemnly filled in the hole and smoothed the surface over.

A crisp brown leaf drifted from the big

sycamore tree and landed on the grave. Sarah sobbed loudly and her mother put an arm round her.

"Thanks for everything, Mike," Carole said. "Wherever Soldier is now, I'm sure he's in a much happier place. Come on, you lot, let's go home."

"Well, I think we can safely say that Mr Harding's not going to come for Jessie tonight," Bob Parker announced late that evening. "I've just tried the phone number he gave us. I got the 'number unobtainable' sound, so I checked with the operator. It's 'out of order', according to her."

Neil bit his lip. Should he tell his dad what he and Kate had found out about Harding's address?

For the moment he decided to keep quiet. He wanted to work it out himself, and with everything else that had happened, the matter of 149 Dale End Road had slipped his mind. Anyway, they had all felt so positive that Harding *would* be back to pick up Jessie.

"What do we do now, then?" Neil enquired.

"Wait to see if he turns up tomorrow. His flight's probably been delayed."

Neil hoped his father was right – that it wasn't anything more serious than that.

Neil spent the following morning working on a school project. There was still no sign of Harding. At lunchtime, he decided to pay Jessie another visit, in case Harding came for her that afternoon and he didn't see her again. When he reached her pen, he got a terrible shock. There was a Yorkshire terrier in it instead of Jessie.

Neil ran to the kennel office. His mother was there, typing at the keyboard of the office computer.

"Where's Jessie, Mum?" he demanded.

"We've put her into the rescue centre," she replied, looking at him over the top of the screen, an edge of weariness in her voice.

"No! You can't! She's not homeless!"

"We had no alternative, Neil. The kennels are fully booked, so we couldn't keep her where she was."

Neil didn't protest. He couldn't. He knew that what his mother said was right: if someone had booked a place for their dog, then Jessie had to move out to make room for it.

"Don't worry, Neil. You know she'll get just the same care and attention. Think of it as just a change of hotel room."

Neil smiled, already feeling a bit better. "Yeah, OK, Mum. I'll go over and see her. Take her for a walk, maybe."

"Don't tire her, will you? Let her dictate the pace. She'll tell you when she's had enough and wants to go home," his mother told him.

"Sure. See you later."

Jessie appeared to be settling into her new

quarters very well. When Neil arrived she was scratching and circling, building herself a really comfortable bed.

"Jessie, walkies," Neil called.

The dog looked up from her exertions and gave a little bark.

Neil unclipped her lead and opened the pen. Jessie sniffed at her handiwork, then walked obediently over to Neil.

It seemed a bit unfair not to take Sam, too. Neil knew he had been neglecting him slightly since Jessie's arrival. He called Sam's name and the Border collie came darting up to him.

The three of them were just crossing the courtyard when Chris stormed around the corner and through the side gate on his bike. He braked so violently that he skidded on the gravel stones before coming to a stop.

"Neil, quick! You've got to see this!" he shouted.

"See what?"

"Something totally weird I've just found. Something you're not going to believe!"

Chapter Eight

"**I**s it far?" Neil asked Chris. "Only I don't want to walk Jessie too far in her condition."

"In the woods," Chris said. "On the other side of the hill. I rode the long way back, down the road, but this way through the fields should be quicker."

Chris was leading the way on foot, with Neil following and keeping a close eye on Jessie. She seemed fine, keeping pace with Sam and even dashing off with him on one of his forays into a nearby hedge.

Neil could not get any information out of Chris about what he was taking him to see. All of his queries about whether it was connected to Soldier met with stony silence and a "Wait and see."

Chris took him to a thick patch of hilly woodland bordering an isolated house. They had never explored round there because the owners of the house had a dog with an exceedingly angry bark. It always seemed best to steer clear.

"It's just up here," said Chris.

"It's very steep," said Neil. "I think I'll leave Jessie here rather than dragging her up this hill. Those mossy stones look really slippery. I wouldn't want her to fall."

He put Jessie's lead on and fastened it securely to a branch. She whined wistfully as the others plunged upward through the trees without her.

It was hard going. "What were you doing up here in the first place?" Neil asked.

"I was on the top road. There are some great paths up here for biking. Then I found—"

"Wow!" Neil interrupted, having suddenly glimpsed what Chris was about to show him. "How on earth did *that* get there?"

That was a white van. It was newish too – not some old wreck that had been rotting in the woods for ages. Neil could see the dents and scratches it had suffered in its wild tumble down the slope. Gouged tree-trunks and snapped branches marked its fall quite clearly.

The van was resting at an awkward angle, almost on its roof, pinned in place between some birch trees. "It can't have been here long. Look at the branches. Those breaks are fairly fresh," said Chris. "And it must have come off the lane that leads to the house."

"You don't think there's anyone in it, do you?" Neil was hesitant. He had awful visions of finding a dead body or someone with terrible injuries.

"I hope not," Chris replied grimly.

They pushed through the undergrowth and hauled their way up the steep slope, grabbing on to branches for extra support as the soles of their trainers slipped on the damp rocks. Sam streaked effortlessly over the obstacles and reached the van ahead of them. He stood waiting for them, wagging his tail proudly.

"It's not locked," Chris pointed out. One of the doors had opened in the fall.

Neil paused, pressing his fingers over his lips as he thought hard. "Do you know something?" he said. "This van looks familiar."

"Yeah? From where? Do you reckon it's the one we saw in the High Street?"

"Oh. Possibly. I was thinking more about Harding. He dropped off Jessie in a van like this. I remember noticing it."

"Well, if this *is* his van, where's Harding? He's late picking up Jess, isn't he?" said Chris.

"If he wasn't the businessman he said he was, but a detective investigating some crime – maybe the antiques robberies – then something may have happened to him. I think we'd better take a good look at that van."

"What about fingerprints, though? We don't want to destroy any evidence."

"We won't touch anything. Just look."

Wrapping the bottom of his sweatshirt around his hands, Chris heaved on the door and managed to get it open far enough for them to stick their heads inside. But before they got a chance, Sam had wriggled through into the cab.

He was out again almost instantly, growling, with something in his mouth.

"Ugh!" exclaimed Neil. "What have you got there? It looks like a dead animal!"

Chris had gone rather pale. "It looks more like a scalp," he said.

"Drop, Sam, drop!" Neil ordered and Sam obediently dropped the black, hairy object at his feet.

Neil touched it with his toe, then flipped it over.

"It *is* a scalp!" Chris said, recoiling in horror.

"No, it's not! It's some sort of wig. Look . . ."

He picked it up with his fingertips and held it out to Chris. Up close, they could see the artificial webbing which the shiny black hair was attached to. With a chill, almost uncanny sense of certainty, something fell into place.

"Perfect shiny black hair . . ." he said. "*Too*

perfect. Remember what I told you Sarah had said about Harding? The day he arrived? She said he had 'funny hair'. I noticed it too. I bet our Mr Harding was wearing a wig, and this is it!"

"A wig? But why would he be wearing a wig?"

"As part of his disguise. If he was a detective—"

"Hey, what if it was Harding driving that van the other night?" Chris broke in. "The driver had ginger hair, but it could still have been him. Maybe this is the van that nearly hit us!"

"Which means he was back in time to pick up Jessie—"

"Or that he never went away at all," Chris said. "Whatever, I bet it's got something to do with that house. We're so close to finding the answer – I can feel it."

"Come on, we've got to look. But we can't leave Jessie. I'll go back and get her," Neil said.

Leaving Chris holding Sam's collar, he scrambled back down the slope. Jessie was pleased to see him. She wagged her tail and gave a short, welcoming bark.

"Come on, girl," Neil told her. "We're going to take this very easily. I don't want you straining yourself."

He took the lead and tried to find the easiest route back to the van. He rejoined Chris and they let the dogs find their own way up, scrambling after them up the rough terrain.

"Sam? Jessie?" Neil called. He was rewarded with some urgent barks which drew them to a spot higher up, past the van, to a wall on which both dogs were standing. A wall with a large hole in it marked with white paint. A trail of churned-up earth and smashed plants led from it.

"At least we know where it came from," said Chris.

Jessie barked suddenly and sniffed the ground on the far side of the wall. She made a dash towards the house.

Close up, the house looked ramshackle. The roof had missing slates and a plant had rooted itself in the gutter. Yet the windows were all intact, not a broken pane amongst them. Chris noticed a burglar alarm set high up on one wall.

Jessie began scratching at the back door, whining and whimpering excitedly.

Chris looked at Neil. "What on earth could be in there that she's so interested in?" he said.

"Rats, probably. Now, how are we going to get into this place?"

"Do you really think we should break in?" queried Chris.

"Only if we have to. C'mon, let's look around."

Ordering Jessie to sit and be quiet, Neil tried the back door handle. The door was locked. They crept cautiously round to the front but there was still no sign of life.

The coast was clear. There was nothing in the front of the house other than a gravel driveway, a badly neglected garden, and a gate which opened on to a muddy, rutted lane with high banks on either side. The front door was as securely locked as the back one.

Then they noticed a sign by the front gate. While Chris tried the door again, Neil went to investigate.

"Hey! It says *Beware Guard Dog*," he told Chris. "There can't be one here, though, or it would have been barking by now."

"What are we going to do?" said Chris. "If we smash a window, we'll set off the alarm. Then we don't know *who* might come dashing up here to see what's going on."

"Looking at the state of that lane, I hardly think anyone will be able to *dash*," Neil replied. "And if the alarm is wired up to the police station, they're just the guys we want to see! Come on, don't be wet. Find a way to get in."

"Those side windows looked old. Maybe one'll be unlocked, or we can force one open." Chris tried a couple of windows without success. "Let's try the front again."

Neil pushed at one of the large sash windows and was relieved when it moved a little. "Success!" he cried. "Give me a hand and we'll be able to make this hole bigger."

Pushing the window together, they soon made the opening big enough for them to climb through.

But before they could move, a streak of brown dog shot past them and leapt through the window. The moment she got inside, Jessie started barking – a wild, excited barking that they had never heard from her before. There was the sound of her paws thudding on wooden stairs. Suddenly the barking stopped.

Neil looked at Chris. "Come on," he said, "We're going in."

Gingerly, they squeezed through the window. Sam put his paws on the windowsill and heaved himself up and through.

They found themselves in the kitchen. The only furniture was a scratched old table and two rickety wooden chairs. A tap dripped monotonously into the cracked and stained enamel sink.

"It's a bit scary, isn't it?" whispered Chris.

Sam followed his nose and padded up the stairs, sniffing at the ground as he went.

Neil nodded. "Scary isn't the word. Where's Sam going? Looks like he's found his tracking instinct at last."

"Come on, let's follow him. Get it over with. Jessie has to be up there."

Holding his finger to his lips, Neil motioned Chris to follow him and they both gingerly crept up the stairs.

There were two doors off the landing, one closed, one half open. Knowing that the dogs must have gone through the open door, they moved towards it. From inside there were muffled noises and some dog sounds, but nothing distinguishable. Chris crept forward first and craned his head around the door to look inside.

Then he stepped back so rapidly that he nearly knocked Neil back down the stairs. "There's a man in there, lying on the floor," he whispered. "The dogs are beside him."

Neither of them said anything as they entered the room.

The man was lying on his side on a filthy, threadbare carpet. He was gagged, with his hands tied behind his back. Sam sat quietly next to him, but Jessie was licking his face ecstatically, her tail waving so fast that it was a blur in the dusty air. The man had ginger hair, but his distinctive, craggy face was familiar.

"Harding!" said Neil.

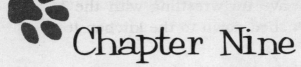 # Chapter Nine

There was a desperate appeal in the eyes of the bound man as he looked straight at Neil and Chris.

"Better get that gag off him. He looks in danger of suffocating," said Chris.

The gag was a grubby black scarf and the knot was tight. Harding moaned and moved his head as Neil worked at untying it.

"I wonder how long he's been here?" Chris looked on anxiously as Neil forced his fingernails into the knot. Harding certainly didn't look like a smart businessman now. His lips were dry and deathly white where the tight material had compressed them, and his face was rough with dark stubble.

Neil gave up wrestling with the knot and Chris rushed down to the kitchen to see if he could find a knife. He came back with a bread knife.

Neil sawed at the knot until the last thread parted.

Harding ran a dry tongue over the cracked skin around his mouth. "Water," he whispered. "Give me water."

This time it was Neil who went down to the kitchen. He filled a chipped mug at the sink but as he did so, he kicked something heavy at his feet. Looking down, he noticed a piece of bubble-wrap sticking out of a half-open cupboard door.

Opening the cupboard, Neil saw four lidless cardboard boxes, each containing articles wrapped in the same protective packaging. He pulled the nearest box out and saw something silver gleaming through the clear bubble-wrap. A thrill shot through him as he reached for the object and gently parted the wrap. He knew nothing about antiques, but the ornate patterning on the silver coffee pot he held in his hands, and the weight of it, convinced him that he held something very valuable.

As he was beginning to think what his

discovery meant, a sound came from the room above him; a heavy, dragging, thumping sound. Neil felt cold prickles of alarm raise all the hairs on the back of his neck. He gripped the mug and ran up the stairs three at a time.

As Neil entered the room, Chris was about to cut the rope which bound Harding's wrists.

"No!" Neil yelled. "Don't untie him!"

Chris looked at Neil as if he were mad. "But he's been tied up for days! He must be in pain."

Harding nodded, his eyes glued to the mug of water. He licked his dry lips. "Please," he said, again in a low, raspy voice.

"It wouldn't do any harm . . ." Chris appealed to Neil.

"We don't know what's happened here yet. We may need to fetch the police."

"How's he going to drink the water?"

"Like this," Neil said. He put the mug on the floor. "Give me a hand."

Together, they tugged the heavy man back into a sitting position with his back against the wall. Jessie promptly leant against him. It was as if she couldn't possibly get close enough to her owner. Neil raised the water to

Harding's lips. He drained the mug in huge, greedy gulps.

"More, please," he croaked, his voice parched from thirst. "I haven't had a thing, food or water, for three days. You haven't got any food, have you?"

"Only these," said Chris, pulling half a packet of mints out of his pocket.

"Untie my hands, boys. Please. I've got no feeling in my fingers," Harding whispered. "Or my feet."

Neil looked down and saw that Harding's ankles were bound with rope too – very tightly.

Jessie whined and nudged her owner. "Just let me stroke my dog," Harding begged in another cracked whisper. "I haven't seen her for a week. She's looking good. You've obviously looked after her well."

Neil felt torn. If it were him lying there, he'd want to give Jessie a proper greeting. What harm would it do to untie him? In such a weak condition, he could hardly run away!

Chris put some mints in Harding's mouth and, as the man began to chew them noisily, Neil picked up the mug and went downstairs to refill it. Chris came after him.

"Look, let's untie him just for a while, so he

can get more comfortable," Chris said. "It seems cruel not to. Half a packet of mints in three days is hardly going to fuel him enough for a two-mile run to Compton. He'd probably collapse! Anyway, he hasn't told us why he's here yet. What if he is working for the police, Neil?"

"Surely he would have told us right away, if he was," Neil pointed out. "He'd have told us where to find his ID. And what about all this stuff?" Neil flicked open the cupboard under the sink to reveal the stash of silver and antique valuables. "How's he going to explain that?"

Chris had a rummage through the boxes and was lost for words. "He's probably still a bit gaga from being tied up," he said after a few moments, ". . . wondering if he was going to starve to death, or die of thirst."

Neil wasn't convinced.

"Let's ask him a few questions, and then make up our minds," Chris suggested.

"OK," Neil agreed.

They took him the water. Again, he swiftly drained it.

"Thanks," he said, his voice a little clearer and stronger.

Neil sat down on the floor, about two feet away from Harding. He crossed his legs and folded his arms. Sam sat obediently by his side. "Right. You obviously haven't been in Tokyo, so what exactly have you been doing?" he demanded.

Harding shook his head. "This and that. Business things," he said.

"What sort of business things get you tied up and dumped in an empty house?" he demanded.

"Not quite empty," Chris reminded him.

"There are a few interesting items downstairs."

Harding groaned as he wriggled and tried to ease his cramped arms. "Now, come on, boys, stop playing games," he said. "Untie me and let me take Jessie home. Then we can talk to the police. What were you intending to do? Go off and leave me here? What if those thugs who tied me up come back for me?"

Neil looked at Chris. Which thugs? Neither of them knew what to do. Then Neil took charge again.

"Those items in the kitchen look like antiques to me," he said. "Could all this have something to do with the robberies that have been taking place recently?"

Neil watched Harding's face closely as he spoke. He gave a slight smile, raised his eyebrows and replied smoothly, "That's very clever of you, kid. You'll grow up to make a good detective."

"Like you?" Chris said.

"Shh!" Neil hissed fiercely. If Harding wasn't a detective after all, then Chris had just put the idea into his head.

"I was right. You're both clever. You've put two and two together and come to exactly the right conclusion. I am a detective. The story

102

about my business trip was a lie and I was indeed investigating the robberies. I was posing as a crooked antiques dealer interested in buying some of the stolen goods cheap," said Harding. His explanation sounded as if it might be true.

"Why did you wear a wig when you brought Jessie to us?" asked Neil.

"There aren't many red-haired detectives around. They'd soon have found out who I was. I'm quite well-known."

"Wouldn't it have been easier to dye your real hair?" Chris enquired.

"Maybe, but not so easy to *keep* it dyed when you're on a case for weeks on end. The wig seemed simpler. But they spotted me without the damn thing on one day, and realized I wasn't all that I seemed."

"What happened?" Chris was beginning to come round to this version of events. He listened intently.

"They were on to me then," Harding continued, "and it was only a matter of time before they discovered through their contacts that I was a detective from the London Met. We had a fight and I ended up here, trussed up like a turkey."

"Why didn't they just kill you, rather than leave you tied up?" Neil asked.

"Killing a policeman is a very serious offence. If they left me here, there was a chance I might be found," Harding explained. "Look, I'm starving, boys. Do I really have to answer all these questions?"

"Only a few more," Neil promised, playing for time while he continued to think about what to do. "Is that your van that we found pushed down the hill?"

"Yes," replied Harding. "After they caught me, they hid it."

"So was that you zigzagging through Compton the other night with a black BMW in tow?"

"Yes. They had a gun. They were after me. I managed to lose them, but they caught up with me later."

"You nearly ran into us!" said Neil, his voice quivering a little. "Didn't you see us?"

"I did at the last moment. I didn't know it was you. Sorry . . ." Harding gave them an apologetic look, then groaned again, shaking his legs. "Come on, get these ankles of mine free. It's vital I contact the police as soon as possible. I'm the only one who knows where the stolen goods are now. I haven't got my mobile, I lost it in the struggle – as I was trying to get away from them. You do believe me, don't you?"

"Go on, Neil," said Chris.

Neil frowned. Harding's story *was* very convincing. A whimper from Jessie made him look down to where she was lying, snuggled up against her owner. She shifted on to her side and began licking at herself. In that position, he could see her swollen belly clearly.

Sam was still sitting nearby on the floor, watching Jessie and Neil.

Harding followed Neil's eyes and saw him looking at Sam. "I remember him from that night I brought Jessie round to you. He looks a smashing dog. By the way, you didn't see a dog outside anywhere, did you? There was a guard dog here."

Chris shook his head. "There was no dog here when we arrived," he said.

"He got hurt in the struggle when the gang captured me. I've been really worried about him."

"What did he look like, this guard dog? Neil's parents run a dog rescue centre, you see, and there's a chance he might have been brought in."

"He was a Dobermann cross. Brown and black. I only saw him the once, when they dragged me here. Called him Brandy."

Harding's words thudded into Neil's brain as he stared at Chris. A wounded black and brown Dobermann cross. The description fitted poor Soldier exactly.

"A dog like that *was* brought into the centre," Neil said slowly.

"He's alive! Great! I've been worried about him. I don't like people harming dogs." Harding smiled for the first time.

"You seem to care an awful lot about a dog you don't even know," said Neil.

Harding said nothing.

Jessie whimpered again.

"The dog's dead," Chris said savagely. "He was shot. He lost a lot of blood. Then he got pneumonia and died."

Harding flinched as if he had been kicked. He blinked several times and his pale face grew even paler. "I tried to stop them," he said. "I tried to make Brandy go for them. When I saw Jamieson point the gun, I tried to deflect the shot. It went wide, but I knew his leg had been hit. All this time I've been hoping he might have got to safety and that he wasn't injured too badly . . ."

Harding's voice choked. Neil stared at him. Instinct was telling him that there was more to it than this. "Why did you try so hard to protect the dog when you were fighting for your own life?" He spoke slowly, trying to get his racing thoughts in some sort of order. "And if he was a guard dog and you were a stranger, why didn't he turn on you? Why should he have obeyed you and attacked them?"

Harding bit his lip and looked away, then met Neil's gaze again.

"OK, OK. I'll tell you. Brandy was my dog. I trained him. I trained both him and Jessie from puppies. I used to be a police dog handler. Jessie's an Airedale cross, the first I ever trained. We found that crossbreeds often trained more easily than pedigrees. Brandy's – I mean, Brandy was . . ."

Harding looked crumpled, but continued. "He was a fantastic animal," he said softly. "He'd do anything for me, obey any order. I was a fool to let them near him. I—"

"Jessie!" The shout from Chris caught everybody's attention.

Neil looked down at Jessie, and crouched down by her side. Jessie's head was down and poked forward. She was panting and her sides were heaving.

"Chris," Neil gasped. "I think her puppies have started!"

Chapter Ten

Harding spoke again, his voice hard and full of authority.

"Right, you two, stop messing around and release me. Come on. This is serious now. Jessie's my dog and her puppies look like they're being born early. If anything happens to them, you'll pay for this!"

"Chris, you get the police and I'll stay here."

"No!" The word exploded into the quiet air of the empty house like a pistol shot. "Just untie me, that's all you need do. We'll get help for Jessie and then we'll go to the police."

Neil glared at Harding and continued giving hurried instructions to Chris. "Tell them that as well as having somebody here that they're looking for, we've also got a dog about to drop. They've got to call dad at the kennels, or Mike Turner."

"I don't understand . . ." Chris stared at Harding with a puzzled expression, then glanced back at Neil. "I thought he was a detective . . ."

"You fell for that story?" Neil tutted and shook his head. "Don't you listen, Chris? Our Mr Harding here dropped himself right in it."

"How?" Chris asked. Harding was keeping quiet, gazing anxiously at the panting Jessie.

"Harding used to be a dog trainer all right, but he was never a detective. Soldier – I mean Brandy – was being used as a guard dog by the thieves. And why doesn't he want us to call the police, eh? I think he wore that wig when he brought Jessie precisely so that the police – or anyone else – wouldn't see him and recognize him. Harding's in this up to his neck."

"But I still don't see—"

"Chris, *go*!"

Chris leapt out of the room and tore down the stairs. Neil heard his footsteps race across the stones outside and clatter down the lane. There was a farmhouse about a quarter of a mile away and Neil guessed he would go straight there to phone.

As soon as Chris had left, Harding seemed to change. His main concern was about Jessie now, rather than his own fate.

"I don't know what's going to happen to me," he told Neil. "Someone's going to have to take care of her. And the pups."

Gone was the smooth wiliness of earlier on. It had been replaced by the type of person Neil could understand: a dog lover.

"OK," he agreed. "So long as you do something for me."

"What's that?" Harding asked, sounding surprised.

"Just tell me the truth. You're not a detective, are you?"

"No."

"You're one of the gang of antiques thieves."

"Yes."

"So what really happened to make them tie you up and dump you?"

Harding heaved a deep sigh. "Greed," he admitted. "I wanted a bigger share of the money for myself, so I tried to double-cross them. I was planning to hijack one of the lorry-loads of stolen goods and make it seem like a police raid. I could have sold it and made a fortune."

Neil whistled. "So you were going to rob the robbers!"

"Yep. I thought I'd won their trust, but I hadn't. They'd been monitoring the calls I made on my mobile while I was finding buyers for the stuff myself. They hid me here while they decided what to do."

"Why did they have to kill Brandy?" Neil wanted to know.

"I told you that dog would have done anything for me. They were worried that I might have got some signal to him to go and fetch help, or something. Or that I might order him to attack them. I could have done both. So it was safest for them to gag me and kill him."

"We gave him a proper funeral, you know," said Neil. "We didn't know his name. We called him Soldier. He's buried in the vet's garden."

"Thanks for telling me that."

Harding gave Neil such a grave, penetrating look that Neil knew he was talking from the heart. There was silence for a few moments as Neil remembered Soldier, and Harding remembered Brandy.

"They were going to come back for that Georgian silver tonight, you know. It's a good job you found me, really. Who knows what they might have done to me."

"So we saved your life?"

Harding nodded. "I suppose a few years in prison is better than being dead."

Jessie's panting stopped for a moment. She looked up at her master and Neil saw the worry in Harding's eyes.

"She'll be all right. Chris will be back soon," he said. "Then we'll get her straight to the kennels."

"If I get banged up in jail, Neil, I'll never see the puppies. It's Jessie's first litter, too. I would have given anything to see those puppies."

Neil bit his lip. It seemed an impossible situation.

They heard the sound of sirens in the distance. "It's the police," said Neil.

"Oh Jess," Harding said, gazing down at the dog lying on the floor. "I'm going to miss you, girl. I'm really going to miss you."

Emily came running out when she saw the police car approaching.

"Go and find Mum or Dad, quick, it's an emergency!" Neil yelled. He climbed out of the back seat, where he had been sitting with Chris and Jessie. He opened the passenger door and Sam bounded out and into the house.

Emily dashed off and soon Bob Parker appeared, a worried look on his face.

"What's wrong? There hasn't been an accident, has there?" he asked the police officer.

"It's Jessie, Dad. Her puppies are coming. They're early."

Bob Parker and Neil lifted Jessie gently from the car. Her sides were rigid and they could feel the spasms as she got ready to push the puppies out.

"We might have to get Mike Turner over – there may be complications. Emily, run and tell your mum about Jessie," Bob said. Then, seeing Neil and Chris climb back into the police car, he exclaimed, "Hey, you two, where are you going?"

"We've got to give statements," Chris told him. "We found Mr Harding. He was one of the antiques robbers."

"You'd better follow us down to the station,

sir," one of the officers told an astounded Mr
Parker. "And we'd better get hold of the other
lad's parents, too."

Giving the statements took a long time. Neil
had to begin his version of events from the
moment Mr Harding brought Jessie to the
kennels. The police wanted to know the exact
time to the minute, so they could try to work
out his movements that evening. They also
wanted to know all about Soldier.

"We've had our eye on Harding for some

time," the Detective Sergeant told them. "He's from Compton originally. His sister still lives here, in Dale End Road."

Chris and Neil looked at one another.

"He went to London and became a dog handler for the Met, but got chucked out for receiving stolen goods – dodgy stereos from a big warehouse raid. He got a suspended sentence. He disappeared for a while after that and we thought he must have gone legit. But we were wrong. Now, tell me exactly where that van is. Oh, and we'll need to collect that wig, for evidence."

All the time they were in the police station, Neil's thoughts were with Jessie. He remembered Harding's words about it being his fault if anything happened to her and the puppies. Perhaps it *was* his fault for having taken her on that walk; for having got her into a situation where she had overdone things; shocking her body into delivering her pups too soon. He couldn't wait to get home and see how she was.

When he finally arrived, his mother said that the puppies still hadn't been born.

Sarah and Emily were allowed to visit Jessie's pen before they went off to bed, but their father wouldn't let them go in. "You mustn't crowd her," he explained. "She needs plenty of space."

He examined Jessie gently while Neil watched with growing anxiety. "I don't like the way she's looking so distressed," he said. "I'm going to give Mike Turner a ring and get him to come and check her over."

Neil sat by Jessie's side, stroking her and talking to her, hardly aware how late it was getting. Soon Emily crept back to join him, wearing an anorak over her dressing gown.

"Mum said I could come. I couldn't sleep worrying about her," Emily whispered.

It was almost ten-thirty when Mike Turner strode into the centre with Mr and Mrs Parker. Neil and Emily moved out of Jessie's pen so that he could examine her.

"I don't think these pups are early," he said. "They seem full size to me. The first pup is the biggest one and it feels as if it's got stuck. That's why nothing's happening. As this is her first litter, I'd feel happier doing a Caesarean."

"What's that?" Emily asked.

"It's an operation to take the puppies out," said Mike. "It's sometimes necessary when the mother isn't able to give birth by herself."

Everyone exchanged anxious glances.

"Don't worry," Mike said. "It's a common operation, and Jessie will soon recover. I'll have to take her back to the surgery with me, though."

"Do you have to?" Neil pleaded.

"It really would be safer for Jessie and easier for me," Mike replied. "We've got special equipment and drugs back at the ops room. I hope I won't need them, but they're there in case I do."

Neil watched Jessie being carried out to Mike's Range Rover. Even though she was a large dog, on the special stretcher Mike used she looked frail and very poorly.

"I'll let you know as soon as there's any news," called Mike, waving to them from the open window of his vehicle as he pulled away.

"OK, let's shut up shop," said Mr Parker as they watched the tail lights of the vehicle disappear. "Jessie's in good hands, now. Worrying about her is not going to help her one bit."

The following day the holidays were over and Neil had to go back to school. He didn't know how he got through his lessons that day.

Twice his teachers had to tell him to pay attention and, to make matters worse, Mr Hamley gave him an extra essay to write for homework, on the subject of daydreaming.

When he finally got home after that endless day, he found the rest of his family sitting round the kitchen table. His mother and father had mugs of coffee and Sarah and Emily were drinking fizzy orange. None of them looked the slightest bit anxious or depressed.

Neil frowned. "Hey, what's with you lot?" he said accusingly. "How could you look happy when poor Jessie's going through a horrible operation!"

He felt a real outsider as they all looked at one another and grinned.

"We know something you don't!" Sarah piped up.

"Come on, let's put him out of his misery," his mother said. "She's had three puppies, Neil. Two bitches and a dog. Mother and babies all doing well, as they say. We're celebrating!"

"When can I see them?" Neil asked excitedly.

"Jessie's going to stay at the vet's tonight,

just to make sure that there are no last-minute complications, but we can collect her tomorrow."

"Yes!" Neil punched the air with excitement. "I must tell Chris," he yelled, racing towards the telephone.

When Neil got home from school the following afternoon, he went straight to the rescue centre. His mother told him where to find Jessie. They had made up a special maternity pen for her.

His father was already there, having just given Jessie some food.

Quietly, his heart thudding in excitement, Neil moved into Jessie's pen. The dog lay contentedly on her side, sleepy and warm under the special heat lamp which Bob Parker had hung inside the pen. Nuzzling close to their mother, blind and velvety-skinned, were three fat little puppies.

"They look like moles!" he laughed.

"They'll soon grow their coats, don't you worry," Bob Parker reassured him.

Neil stroked Jessie's head gently.

"Will she be able to feed the puppies OK with that scar?" he asked eventually. He could clearly see the shaved area on her abdomen and the line of stitches from her operation.

"Oh, yes," said his father. "And she'll have the stitches taken out in ten days' time. By that time the pups will probably have their eyes open."

They watched the puppies squirm against Jessie's side, pummelling her with their tiny paws and making little squeaking noises. Jessie turned her head to lick them all again, while they sucked noisily at her teats. One puppy – the largest – kept pushing the others aside.

"That one's going to be a right little bruiser," commented Mr Parker.

"I suppose that's the dog pup," said Neil. He stared at it. Did it have a slight look of Dobermann?

"That's the pup that caused all the trouble. He was too big to come out."

Neil could have stayed there watching for hours, but he had homework to do, so he locked up his bike and went indoors to join Sarah and Emily who were having their tea.

"I hope Jessie and her babies can stay with us for always!" said Sarah.

"I know, honey," said Carole, "but it's just not possible. Her owner's sister has telephoned. She's coming to collect Jessie and the pups as soon as they can be moved."

"She lives in Dale End Road, doesn't she?" Neil asked.

"Yes. Why?" asked his mother.

"You don't by any chance remember which number, do you?"

"I'm pretty sure it was 147. I'll go and check . . ."

She went off to the office and came back with the card. "See? 147. I was right!"

Neil seized the card. "That looks like a nine, not a seven," he observed.

"Yes, it does a bit, doesn't it? But I know it's

a seven. It's my horrible, wiggly writing. Normally, I'd have typed it, but it was so late and I couldn't be bothered switching on the electric typewriter."

Neil sighed, thinking what Kate and Chris were going to say about the clue that never was!

"Harding's sister has asked us to help her find homes for the pups," his mother said.

"He's never going to see them, is he?" Neil said. "He'll be in prison."

"That's where he ought to be, too. He's a crook!" Emily pointed out.

"But he loved Jessie. And Brandy. And they loved him. I don't think anyone who loves dogs can be all that bad," Neil said. "Do you?"

He gazed at the faces of his family, looking from one to the other, daring them to disagree. But nobody did. They all remained silent, even Sarah.

Suddenly, Neil found that he couldn't eat any more, and tossed his half-eaten toast into the rubbish bin. He felt choked. What if Harding spent so long in prison that Jessie grew old and died and he never saw her again?

Just then, Neil felt a familiar wet nose pushing its way into his hand. It was Sam, who had squeezed his way in to see what all the fuss was about and was demanding attention.

Neil shook his head, as if to clear it of all other dogs. He went to fetch his coat.

"Come on, Sam," he said. "You know none of them are as good as you. Tomorrow, we're going to start training you again and next summer you're going to win that Agility course paws down, or I'm not the best dog trainer in Compton!"